On the Seesaw Bridge

Story by Yuichi Kimura   Art by Kowshiro Hata

After many days,
the rain stopped at last.
The heavy rain beat down the bridge,
and it was now just a single log.

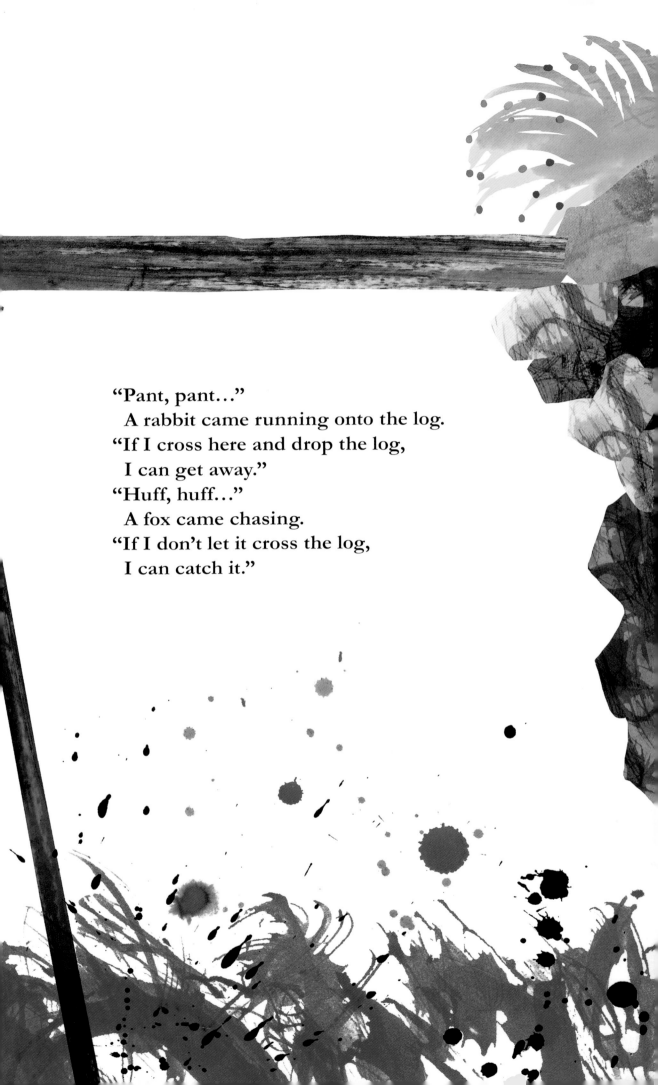

"Pant, pant…"
  A rabbit came running onto the log.
"If I cross here and drop the log,
  I can get away."
"Huff, huff…"
  A fox came chasing.
"If I don't let it cross the log,
  I can catch it."

Whomp

The fox jumped onto the log.
The log bounded wildly,
and the rabbit clung to it with a cry.
The fox grinned
and thumped across the log.
"Ha, I won't let you across so easily."
The rocks on the bank were loose from
the rain and went tumbling down.

The log finally came loose from the bank
and started to seesaw. The fox just smacked
its lips and approached the rabbit.
"Ha ha, you can't run anymore."

Kreee—

Then the bridge began tilting more and more.
"Hey, don't come any closer, or we'll fall into the river with the log," the rabbit shouted.
The fox stopped in haste.
"Oops, this is dangerous."

When the fox hurried and drew back,
the log now tilted the other way.
Every time the fox moved,
the log seesawed.

Lurch

"I'd better watch where I go.
If I fall into these rapids, it's the end."
The fox searched for the right point of balance.

"Tsk. Do I have to sit still
     with my prey in front of me?"
     the fox muttered bitterly.
     The rabbit glared at the fox and said,
"Hah. I can't run away, either.
     But my friend will come and
     shove you down into the river with a pole."

Naturally, the fox answered back.
"When my friend comes,
   we'll share you half and half."

"Hey, somebody!" "Somebody, come!"
   The two shouted with all their might
   at the dusk sky.
   Then…

"Caw. Did you caw-l us?"
"What do you want?"

Crows started to gather and land one after another.
"Humph, we never called for you."
"Oh no, don't all land on this side."
The crows landed where they pleased,
so the log started seesawing again.

"Uh-oh, the sun is gaw-ing down."
"Right, let's hurry home."
  As the crows flapped home across
  the dusk sky,
  the two glared at them and sighed
  together.
"Phew, what a selfish bunch."
"Really, I thought the log would fall."

Time flowed in the quiet, and soon,
night swallowed up the two.

"Aw, I'd rather not spend the night here,"
the fox muttered.

"Yeah, there might be ghosts."

"Stop that. I was a coward
when I was young."

"Ah hah, so foxes get
scared too sometimes."

"Sure. Once you're scared,
even a thicket looks
like a scary face."

"Exactly. Turning around
when nobody's there."

Since they couldn't move,
all the two could do was talk on the log.

"When I've been scared,
I always need to pee."

"Ah hah. Me, I scream
that I'm scared."

Forgetting that they're enemies, the two talked and talked.
About their siblings, the cold of winter, the fun they had…

Suddenly, the rabbit stopped answering.

The fox listened closely and heard the rabbit's faint snoring.

The fox shouted loud and clear.

"Hey, rabbit! Wake up. Don't sleep now, or you'll fall and die. Come on! **Value your life more!!**"

"Oh, thanks. I've woken up. Ya~wn.
Say, isn't it strange?
You were trying to eat me before.
Now you want me to value my life."
"Yeah, think about it.
If you fall, this log will tilt and..."

"Ha ha, you're right. We need
each other's weight at the moment."
When the rabbit said so, the two noticed
that the bridge was seesawing.

The dawn wind blowing down from the mountains
was getting stronger. Whooooosh!
Stirred by the wind, the log slowly started to turn.
"Hey, rabbit! Don't fall."
"I know. Don't you let go, either."
The two clung onto the log desperately.

As the log spun, their bodies slid to its ends…

"Waah, I can't hold on!!"

"I-I'm going to fall!!?"

Just then…

Sssszap
The fox's legs got caught
in a thicket on the bank.
"Rabbit, now!! Hurry and cross!"
"Okay!"
With a hop, the rabbit crossed
over the fox's back.

"Here, grab tight."
"All right."
  Grabbing the rabbit's hands,
  the fox climbed onto the bank as well.
  Right at that moment!!

Splash!

A column of water shot up behind them.
The log had fallen into the river.
"Phew, we're safe."
"Whoa, that was scary."
Without thinking, the two congratulated
each other. But then…

In a blink, the fox became
its old self again. Its eyes glinted.
"Oops, look out."
The rabbit leapt off the ground
and started running for dear life.
"Wait!!" Of course the fox chased after it,
but stopped all of a sudden, saying,
"Ah, I need to pee after
I've been scared, don't I?"

Taking his time to pee,
the fox called out in a small voice,
"Hey rabbit! Don't ever get caught!!"

ABOUT THE AUTHORS

Yuichi Kimura is a versatile writer who has penned scripts for picture and comic books, television, and the stage. *One Stormy Night*, for which he won the Sankei Children's Publishing Culture Award and the Kodansha Publishing Culture Award, is also available in English translation (Kodansha International).

Kowshiro Hata is an illustrator and designer. He has drawn picture books for major Japanese publishers. Many of his works have been translated and loved around the world.

Text © 2003 by Yuichi Kimura
Illustrations © 2003 by Kowshiro Hata

Translation © 2011 by Vertical, Inc.

All rights reserved.

Published by Vertical, Inc., New York.

Originally published in Japanese as *Yurayura-bashi no ue-de* by Fukuinkan Shoten Publishers, Inc., Tokyo, 2003.

ISBN 978-1-935654-18-6

Manufactured in Malaysia

First American Edition

Vertical, Inc.
451 Park Avenue South, 7th Floor
New York, NY 10016
www.vertical-inc.com